Just for Fun

A Collection of Stories & Verses

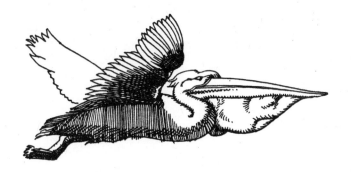

Just for Fun

A Collection of Stories & Verses

ILLUSTRATED BY
Robert Lawson

DOVER PUBLICATIONS, INC.
Mineola, New York

Acknowledgments

To Carol Johnstone Sharp for "Auntie Grumble Meets the Wizard"; to Beatrice Curtis Brown for "Jonathan Bing Does Arithmetic," "More About Jonathan Bing," and "Jonathan Bing Dances for Spring" from the book, *Jonathan Bing and Other Verses*, published by Oxford University Press, New York and London; to Mildred Plew Meigs for "The Pelican"; to Laura E. Richards for "The Wogg and the Baggle," and to Laura E. Richards and Little, Brown & Company for "Story Tell" from *Tirra Lirra*; to Padraic Colum and The Macmillan Company, publishers, for "The Man with the Bag" from *The Big Tree of Bunlahy*; to Eunice Tietjens for "St. Valentine"; to Constance Savery and Longmans, Green & Company for "The Little Dragon"; to Nancy Byrd Turner for "Planting a Tree"; to Anne Brewer for "Penguins"; and to Florence Page Jaques for "The Piping on Christmas Eve."

Bibliographical Note

This Dover edition, first published in 2013, is an unabridged republication of the work originally published by Rand McNally & Company, New York, in 1940.

Library of Congress Cataloging-in-Publication Data

Lawson, Robert.
   Just for fun : a collection of stories and verses / Robert Lawson.
       v. cm.
   "This Dover edition, first published in 2013, is an unabridged republication of the work originally published by Rand McNally & Company, New York, in 1940."
       Summary: A collection of thirteen tales and rhymes featuring wizards, dragons, and princes in disguise by Padraic Colum, Beatrice Curtis Brown, Eunice Tietjens, and others with more than forty pen-and-ink drawings.
       Contents: Auntie Grumble meets the wizard / by Carol Johnstone Sharp — Jonathan Bing does arithmetic / by Beatrice Curtis Brown — The pelican / by Mildred Plew Meigs — The wogg and the baggle / by Laura E. Richards — The man with the bag / by Padraic Colum — More about Jonathan Bing / by Beatrice Curtis Brown — St. Valentine / by Eunice Tietjens — Story tell / by Laura E. Richards — The little dragon / by Constance Savery — Planting a tree / by Nancy Byrd Turner — Jonathan Bing dances for spring / by Beatrice Curtis Brown — Penguins / by Anne Brewer — The piping on Christmas Eve / by Florence Page Jaques.
   ISBN-13: 978-0-486-49720-4 (pbk.)
   ISBN-10: 0-486-49720-8
   1. Children's literature. [1. Literature—Collections.] I. Title.

PZ5.L526Ju 2013
[E]—dc23

                                                                                    2012051310

Manufactured in the United States by Courier Corporation
49720801   2013
www.doverpublications.com

Contents

Just for Fun

A Collection of Stories & Verses

Auntie Grumble Meets the Wizard

By Carol Johnstone Sharp

FROM all directions the little people of Vilville came running to the Round Square. There stood the town notice board, as usual, but what was most unusual, there was a notice on it! Such a thing had not happened since dear knows when—at any rate not since the Wizard of Vilville had packed up his magic one day and journeyed away to do a little free-lance wizzing in near-by towns. But here was a notice, and this is what it said:

GOOD PEOPLE, TAKE NOTICE
I shall return to Vilville on Thursday noon. I have disguised myself as a rabbit so that none of you shall know me.
I shall be VERY HUNGRY.
The first person who feeds me shall be granted
A PECULIAR POWER *from noon until six o'clock.*
(*Signed*) THE WIZARD OF VILVILLE

Such hurrying and bustling about, as the Vilvillians and the little Vilvillianesses began to collect food for the Wizard-rabbit, for the very next day would be Thursday! No one was quite sure what the Peculiar Power might be, but they were certain it would be quite magic and nice.

9

Long before noon on Thursday the road that led into Vilville was lined with eager people with arms full of wizard food and
rabbit food and food that no rabbit or wizard could ever, ever eat.
About a quarter of twelve a boy with sharp eyes suddenly began to
jump up and down and scream, "There he comes! I see him!"

All the people looked, and sure enough, down the road
came scampering a brown bunny. Now it just happened that a
little real rabbit who lived in the woods had grown very hungry
that morning, and had decided to venture into the village to look
for a scrap of something to nibble. Of course, the people did not
know that. They were sure this was their Wizard and they began
shouting and rushing toward him with things to eat in their hands.

Well, when the poor little woods bunny looked up and saw
two potatoes, a bag of peas, and a lamb chop come flying through
the air, he dodged, jumped ahead—and found himself right in the
midst of a crowd of excited people all tossing food at him.

"Here Wizzy! Wizzy! Wizzy!" shrieked a dozen voices.

"Take mine! Take mine!"

10

"No, mine! You'll like mine better!"

"Open your mouth, bunny, and I'll throw it in!"

The rabbit's ears stood right up on end with fright.

"For goodness sake!" he thought. "Is *everybody* in this place crazy? If I don't get out of here, I'll certainly die of overfeeding!"

So he hopped wildly from one spot to another, dodged a chicken sandwich, a pot of coffee, a basket of spinach, and two bowls of soup and finally gave one great leap over the head of a puffing old woman who was thrusting a rice pudding at him.

Jump, jump, and away! As fast as any rabbit could hop, he dashed right through the middle of the town and down the far end of the street. After him streamed the entire crowd of Vilvillians, calling and shouting and dropping their food gifts along the way as they ran. Not a soul was left in the village!

That is, there was no one left except old Auntie Grumble, who lived in the Last Street. The most unpleasant person! To begin with, she did not care a bit for magic, and didn't believe in the Wizard at all, though she had seen him in half a dozen disguises and had recognized him every time! She was so cross and disagreeable that no one paid much attention to her, and no one even thought of her today. So there she was, left alone in her crooked old house, complaining to herself as usual in her grumpy way.

"All that commotion!" she grumbled. "People racing through the town! Wizard—humph! As if there *were* wizards! Best food, too—all this racket and bother—street littered with food—" Mumbling and muttering, Auntie Grumble hobbled out to her front gate.

"And just see that!" she complained, stooping to pick something off the ground. "Here's a carrot some careless person dropped—makes my gateyard look as bad as the rest—*trash!*" And very crossly Auntie Grumble threw the carrot as far out into the road as she could.

11

But while the people were chasing a scared little woods bunny out of the other side of town, and while Auntie Grumble was hobbling angrily back into her house, where was the Wizard of Vilville?

Yes, *where* do you suppose he was?

Why, he was loping slowly into the village, disguised as a rabbit, wondering what on earth had happened to his old friends the Vilvillians. He looked about him amazed, for the houses and streets were empty. There was no sound in the little green yards, although he thought he heard a far-off commotion beyond the other end of the village. But not a soul did he see. It actually seemed as if nobody cared whether he came to town or not!

He hopped along, growing more annoyed at every step. He was about to become hopping mad! "So that's how it is!" he exclaimed. "If they do not care any more for me than this, then I *will* go away and never do another wiz for them, ever, ever again. Here I am, nearly starving, and—"

WHOP!

The Wizard leaped into the air as a great big luscious carrot hit him right between the ears. And who do you suppose had thrown it?

You're right! Auntie Grumble!

Hungrily the Wizard fell upon that lovely carrot and began to nibble it, forgetting how vexed he had been a moment before. As the last sweet bit slid down his little red lane he wiped his whiskers, twitched his nose, and went hop-hopping up to Auntie Grumble's house. There he found old Auntie seated on a stool, scowling and scolding to herself.

The Wizard bowed until his ears touched the floor.

"Many thanks, good lady, for the delicious food!" he said to her very politely.

Auntie Grumble looked up and squinted her eyes at him.

"And who are you?" she demanded.

"What do I look like?" asked the Wizard, surprised.

"You look like a rabbit, of course!"

"Good!" said the Wizard with satisfaction. "I have disguised myself as a rabbit purposely to look like one. I'm glad it works!"

"Oh, then you must be—" Auntie Grumble could not say "the Wizard" because she thought she did not believe in wizards.

"Why, Madam, I am the Wizard of Vilville!" announced the rabbit proudly. He bowed again.

"Now I must grant you the Peculiar Power, as advertised on the town notice board. Gizzick! Gizzock! Gizzook! There, my good lady; you have it."

"Have what?" said the old woman.

"The Peculiar Power. From now until six o'clock, if you say it is—it is! Just remember that, and use it wisely, please. Now I must be hopping along. Good day!"

"Now what on earth did that rabbit mean?" said Auntie

Grumble when the Wizard had gone ka-hop, ka-hopping out of sight.

"Well, if I have any Peculiar Power it isn't hurting me anywhere. 'If I say it is, it is!' The idea! Such talk! Well, I must go and get a broom—can't tell what gets tracked in—rabbits all over the house like this—"

Old Auntie Grumble stopped suddenly and began screaming, "Eeee! Eeee! Eeee!" For in just that moment the house *was* full of rabbits, just as she had said—although she hadn't meant exactly that, really. But she had said it. The Peculiar Power worked!

And now what was she to do with all these rabbits? Here they were, hopping madly all over the house, scurrying under the beds, leaping over the chairs, scampering into every corner, and having the best time! Old Auntie seized her broom and began waving it wildly about, chasing the rabbits out of the house. They gave her a merry run of it before they finally fled through the door—and if rabbits really do laugh, then every one of those bunnies was certainly giggling as he ran. Poor Auntie Grumble sat down panting and gasping.

"Now, whatever made that happen?" she sighed, fanning herself with her apron. "Just look at my hands, chasing those dirty animals under the furniture. I'll have to wash them—they are simply black!"

Ugh! Ugh! What a funny feeling, creeping over her hands! She looked at them quickly, and then even more quickly she hid them under her apron and looked up at the ceiling, pretending she had not seen anything unusual at all. But just the same, she was terribly startled, for her hands certainly—were—black!

Outdoors the Vilvillians were coming slowly back into town. Poor people! They looked so downhearted. After getting ready such nice things to eat, and after chasing that bunny all over

the place, here it had not been the Wizard at all! Perhaps, they thought, the Wizard never *would* come back now! Sadly they carried home what was left of their food gifts.

Auntie Grumble leaned out of her window. "Humph!" she said jerkily. "Here they all come, tired out for nothing. They ought to hurry home where they belong—it'll be raining cats and dogs in a minute."

Sixty seconds passed.

And then, to be sure, the air was suddenly full of little furry or hairy things that came plumping down to the ground crying, *"Yipe! Yipe!"* and *"Meow! Meow!"* and *"Ffft! Ffft!"* and *"Bow-wow-wow!"*

It was raining cats and dogs!

The commotion was dreadful. Everyone scampered for shelter, holding his hands over his ears to keep out the awful racket that all those live raindrops were making. They bounced to the ground, rolled over one another, barked and mewed—and kept right on coming down!

The old woman who had caused all the fuss found herself jumping up and down in her excitement, and before she realized it she was exclaiming, "No, it isn't! No, it isn't! It isn't raining anything!"

Ssssh! The noise stopped just as suddenly as it had begun, and not a single other cat or dog or kitten or pup fell from the sky. And as fast as they could, every little boy in Vilville ran out and caught a cute puppy for himself, and each little girl captured a kitty for her very own, and the rest all scampered away.

But now old Auntie Grumble had to sit down and think

16

it over. There was no use denying it any longer. She cer-tain-ly had a Peculiar Power! And who had given it to her but the rabbit who had called himself the Wizard of Vilville? Well, well, well; maybe it was true, after all. But how should she use it wisely, as the rabbit had said?

She rocked and puffed and winked and snuffed and tapped her toes and wrinkled her nose and tried to think. It was true that she was a very unhappy old woman. She disliked everybody, and of course everybody disliked her. When anyone tried to be nice to her she only frowned and mumbled. She was so snappish with children that they ran to hide if they saw her coming. It was no wonder that Auntie Grumble was unhappy. But then, it actually seemed as if she *liked* to be that way!

As she sat rocking and shaking her head and being sorry for herself, the strangest thought came to her! Perhaps it was the Peculiar Power doing a little work on its own account. Anyway, Auntie Grumble suddenly had the feeling that she wanted to be happy! Oh, how much she wanted to be happy! She actually felt she had to do something about it right away!

"If I say it is, it is! Well, why not?" suddenly exclaimed Auntie Grumble, leaping from her chair and walking to her door. "I might as well give the thing a try, anyway." She smoothed her apron, patted her hair into place, folded her arms across her middle, and standing quite still she said soberly, *"I am very happy!"*

And then, "Oh-h-h!" she exclaimed, in the sweetest, most delighted tone of voice. "How lovely, how beautiful, how—how *happy* everything is!" She looked up and down and all about her, tilting her head this way and that, and noticing for the first time that there were birds on the roof, pinky flowers growing along the fence, and soft green moss snuggled about the foot of the tree near her doorstep.

Auntie Grumble felt so lighthearted and brand-new, some-

17

how, that she found herself laughing out loud. She laughed and shook and shook and laughed, and all the frown-wrinkles on her face began to crack into pieces and fall to the ground with a curious little tinkling sound. She kept on laughing until the windows of the house began to jiggle and jingle, and the shingles on the roof started slapping and clapping, and the tree fluttered its leaves, and the birds opened their little beaks and began to sing in time to the funny little music dance that was going on. It just sounded too jolly for anything!

You may believe that it was not very long before children began peeking over the gate, and older people came cautiously into the little yard to see what all this odd music was about.

"Can that be Auntie Grumble? She seems so changed!" someone whispered.

"Yes, it is really she. But what has happened?"

And now came the greatest surprise of all that surprising day.

"Good afternoon, dear neighbors!" said Auntie Grumble, most cheerfully! She had finally stopped laughing, but her face was still sweet and merry. "While you were off chasing a woods bunny, the Wizard of Vilville came to my house, disguised as a rabbit."

"Oh-h-h!" gasped the Vilvillians, opening their eyes very wide.

"By the merest chance," went on the old lady, "I was the first to feed him. In return for a single carrot, he granted me the Peculiar Power!"

"Ah-h-h-h!" whispered the people of Vilville.

"He told me this, 'If you say it is—it is!'"

"Wha-a-at?" they said.

"And he told me to use it wisely. I—I guess I haven't used it very wisely," the old lady said, smiling a little bashfully.

18

"You see, I made it rain cats and dogs awhile ago, but that was quite an accident. And look! This was an accident too!" She held up her hands for the people to see, and of course they were still pitchy, pitchy black.

"I will show you how the Power works, if you like. See! My hands are *white!*" In a flash the black vanished, and her hands were gleaming white again.

"Oh, wonderful! Wonderful!" cried the people.

"But now, good neighbors, I think I have found a way to use the Peculiar Power wisely, as the Wizard told me. If you will hurry up and tell me your troubles, I shall do my best to make you all happy. But please do not delay."

The people all began chattering at once, and clamoring to be the first to be heard by Auntie Grumble. They were trying to discover a lot of troubles for her to set right, and they made a terrible racket about it. It took them so long to become orderly that suddenly Auntie Grumble threw up her hands in dismay.

"Oh! Oh! Oh!" she cried. "It is six o'clock, and the Peculiar Power is—is—oh dear! It *isn't* any more! It was only supposed to last until six o'clock!" She picked up her apron and began to wipe her eyes, for there were big tears rolling from them.

The people, startled and ashamed of their clamor, stopped their noise and whispered uncertainly among themselves. What had they done?

Then a plump old man with jolly whiskers stepped out of the crowd and climbed the steps beside Auntie Grumble.

"Now, now, now! Do cheer up, good folks!" he said in a most jovial tone. "Our nice Wizard has come back to us again, and aren't we happy over that?"

"Of course," said the people, a little doubtfully.

"And really," the old man went on, "you know that not a single one of us has any real-for-sure-enough troubles. So why should we need a Peculiar Power to make us any better off? Why, the only thing in Vilville that needed a little fixing was Auntie Grumble's grumble. And look at her now. Isn't she the sweetest, cheerfullest old lady you ever saw?"

The people looked. They smiled—they began to laugh with pleasure, and all of a sudden they were cheering for pleasant old Auntie.

The next day, everybody was crowding about the Town Notice Board again, talking in excited, happy tones about a new notice that was posted there—a message to the Wizard this time:

Dear, Good Wizard!
Thank you! Thank you!
Please come to Vilville soon again.
(signed) *Auntie* GENTLE
(*who used to be called Auntie Grumble*)

Jonathan Bing
Does Arithmetic

By Beatrice Curtis Brown

WHEN Jonathan Bing was young, they say,
He shirked his lessons and ran away,
Sat in a meadow and twiddled his thumbs
And never learnt spelling or did any sums.

So now if you tell him, "Add 1 to 2,"
"I don't understand!" he'll answer you;
"Do you mean 2-day or that's 2 bad?
And what sort of 1 do you want me to add?

"For there's 1 who was first when the race was 1,
Though perhaps 2 many were trying to run,
So if 2 had 1 when the race was through,
I'd say the answer was 1 by 2!"

O Jonathan Bing, you haven't the trick
Of doing a sum in arithmetic!

The Pelican

By Mildred Plew Meigs

OH, the pelican's a model
  Never noted for his looks,
But all the same his noddle
  Has a lot of clever nooks!
Now the ostrich, one of many,
  Wears a pretty feather fan,
Yet he couldn't tell a penny
  From a new tin pan;
  But the pelican,
    The pelican,
      The pelican can,
For the pelican's a wise old bird;
And though he's so absurd,
  When he goes to make a plan,
  You'll notice that the pelican can!

Oh, the pelican he doesn't
   Have a hover like a hawk,
And people say he wasn't
   Ever noted for his talk!
Now the parrot with his chatter
   Will divert you for a span,
Yet he couldn't spin a platter
   On a pink divan;
   But the pelican,
      The pelican,
        The pelican can,
For the pelican's a wise old bird;
And though he's never heard
   To end what he began,
   It's certain that the pelican can!

Robert
Lawson

The Wogg and the Baggle

By Laura E. Richards

THAT amiable entity
   called the Wogg
Was sitting one day
   on a lumpety log
When a Baggle came out
   of the woodland wild
And said, "Will you be
   my Orphan Child?

"Now do! I'll dress you
   in satin and silk,
You shall sup (if you like it)
   on Muggery Milk,
And all the daylight
   so live and long,
We'll sit together
   and sing this song.

24

"Hey, the Baggle!
And ho, the Wogg!
Neither of us
Resembles a frog,
Neither resembles
   in the least
Fishkin or fleshkin,
   bird or beast.
Therefore how happy
   we both should be,
Tinkery tonkery,
   twee wee wee!"

The Wogg replied,
   "Your hair's in a snaggle,
Yet you seem to be
   rather a winsome Baggle.

"It might be pleasant,
   and wholesome, too,
To sit and quaver
   a song with you.

"But my parent Woggs
   live over the hill,
They're always afraid
   of my getting a chill;

25

"And under the Ging-tree
    over the way
Squatters my grandmother
    old and gray.
So though your manners
    are milky mild,
I never can be
    your Orphan Child.

"So hey, the Baggle!
    And ho, the Wogg!
Though neither of us
    Resembles a frog;
Though neither resembles
    in the least
Fishkin or fleshkin,
    bird or beast,
The song you never
    can hear from me,
Of tinkery tonkery,
    twee wee wee."

The Man with the Bag

By Padraic Colum

ONCE upon a time a man who had a beggar's bag on his back came to the door of a house that was hereabouts. He asked for shelter. "And if you let me take my rest here while I'm begging through the parish I'll ask you for nothing else, ma'am," said he to the woman of the house. "A good beggar doesn't ask for food where he gets shelter and doesn't ask for shelter where he gets food. I know what a good beggar's conduct should be. My father was a beggar and his father was a beggar before him. I'm no upstart."

The woman of the house told him he could rest by the fire when he finished his round of begging in the evening, and when she told him this the man with the bag on his back turned from the door and went along the crooked lane that went from the house.

The woman's daughter was there, and she looked after him as he went down the laneway. And she thought that only for the grime that was on him and the ragged clothes that he wore he would be good-looking enough. Let the beggarman go on while I tell you about the girl. She was named Liban, and well did she deserve the name which means Beauty of Woman, for her eyes were beaming, her mouth was smiling, her cheeks were like roses, and her hair was brown as a cluster of nuts. But for all her

27

beauty Liban had little chance of being wedded. Young men came to ask for her in marriage, but if they did, her mother told them they were first to climb the tree that overhung the high cliff, and take out of the raven's nest that was there a scissors that the raven had carried off, and bring

back in addition two of the raven's eggs. One young man and another young man would climb the tree, but when he came to the top branches that overhung the cliff and found them breaking under him, he would get down from the tree and not go to the door of the house again. So Liban stayed and was likely to stay beside her mother's hearth, spinning threads on her spindle while her mother spun them upon her wheel. And this was just what her mother wanted her to be doing, for she got a deal of silver for all the thread that she and Liban spun.

The beggarman came back in the evening and his bag hung as if there were nothing in it. All the same, he refused the milk and bread that Liban offered him. "All that I'll take in your house," said he, "is the place to rest myself, and leave to put in your charge what I get on my travels." And saying that he put his hand down into the bag, and searched and searched there, and brought up what he found. It was a pea. "I'll leave this in your charge and you'll be accountable for it," said he. "I'll take it back from you when I'm going." She took the pea and put it on the corner of her spinning wheel. Then the beggarman put the bag under his head and went to sleep by the fire.

Liban and her mother came out of the sleeping room at the peep of day, and as they did the beggarman got up from where he was lying, and opened the house door, and went off on his rounds with the crooked lanes of the parish before him. Liban went to get ready for breakfast. The little speckled hen that was her own came in to pick up the crumbs that would be around the table. But when she came as far as the spinning wheel she saw the pea, and when she saw it she picked it and swallowed it.

"Mother," Liban said, "the pea that the beggarman left in your charge, my own little speckled hen has swallowed."

"He'll forget to ask about it," said her mother, "and as for you, take the spindle and get some threads done while the breakfast porridge is cooling."

The first thing the beggarman said when he came in was, "Where is the pea I left in your charge, woman of the house?"

"A hen ate it."

"Which is the hen that ate the pea I left in your charge?"

"The speckled hen that's before you."

"If the speckled hen ate the pea that was mine, the hen herself is mine."

"That cannot be."

"It can be and it is, ma'am. It's the law, and if a beggarman doesn't know the law, who would know it?"

29

And saying this he took up the hen that was picking from a dish on the floor and put her into his empty bag. And the woman of the house believed what he said, for she had once stood in a court—the Court of Dusty Feet it was—and had heard a sentence passed on a man who had lost something that was left in his charge and that he was accountable for.

When the beggarman was going off the next morning he took the speckled hen out of his bag. "I leave her in your charge," he said to Liban's mother.

Then he went off, facing the crooked lanes of the parish, his empty bag hanging on his back. And Liban, so that nothing might happen to her, made a little pen of wattles for the speckled hen, and tied her inside of it. Then she took up her spindle and her mother went to her wheel. "I wish that beggarman had come to ask you in marriage so that I might have made him climb the tree," she said.

Liban was looking out of the door. She saw the pig beside the pen of wattles. The pen was strange to the pig, and she went rooting around it. The speckled hen flew into her mouth. The pig ate her. All that was left of the little speckled hen was the white feathers on the pig's snout.

And the first thing that the beggarman said when he came in on the door was, "Where is the speckled hen that I left in your charge?"

"The pig ate her," said Liban's mother.

"Then the pig is mine. That's the law, and if a beggarman doesn't know the law, who'd know it?" He went out to the yard and took the pig by the leg and dragged her into the house. He put her into his bag and tied up the mouth of his bag. Then he went to sleep by the fire.

By the time that the beggarman went out of her door next morning, Liban's mother had lost so much flesh through grief at the

31

loss of her pig that she looked as if the weight of a pig had been taken out of her. And she wasn't able to eat her porridge either. Liban took charge of the pig. She tied her to a bush under a wall of loose stones, thinking no harm could come to her there. Then she went back to her spinning. But before she had more than a few threads spun, the horse galloping towards the house threw the stones of the wall down upon the pig. Then, trying to get up from where he was lying, the horse struck out with his hoofs and killed the pig. When Liban and her mother raised the horse up they found the pig with her head split open.

"Every misfortune has come on us since that beggarman came to the house for shelter. He'll want to take our horse now. If he does and rides away on him, I'll be content with my loss—so glad I'll be to see the last of the beggarman."

He came back in the evening with a corner of his bag filled.

"Where's my pig?"

"Our horse has killed her."

"Your horse is mine."

"Take him and ride away, and may all my bad luck go with you."

"No. I never stay less then five days in any house. It's due to a promise I made to my father. He feared that I might become a vagabond, one day here and another day there, and he made me promise I'd stay the greater part of the week in any house I had been given shelter in. One day more I'll stay for the sake of the promise I made. Mind the horse for me—I put him in your charge."

He lay by the fire, his head on his bag, and he went to sleep. The next morning he went off, his bag on his back, and his face towards the crooked lanes of the parish. Liban put a halter on the horse, and, so as not to let him get into any danger, went with him everywhere the horse went to graze. Along the cliff he went where the grass was sweetest. When they came to the tree that the raven's nest was in, Liban put her hands before her eyes so that she might look up and see how high the young men had to climb when they had asked for her. Not so high at all, she thought. And there was the raven on the branch above the nest, flapping her wings at her. As she looked, the horse, leaning out to get a mouthful of sweet grass, slipped and slithered down the cliff. And the raven with a croak flew down after him.

So poor Liban went back to her mother's. "Our horse is gone now," she said. "Over the cliff he has fallen, and what will the beggarman take from us now?"

"Nothing at all can he take," said her mother. "Let him take the horse's skin, and come next nor near us no more."

When he came back that evening with only a corner of his bag filled, the beggarman said, "Where's my horse so that I can go riding tomorrow?"

"The horse fell over a cliff and the raven is upon him now."

"Who was minding my horse when he fell over the cliff?"

"My daughter was minding your horse."

"Then your daughter is mine. That's the law, and if you don't think it is the law I'll stand face to face with you about it in

the Court of Dusty Feet." And saying this the beggarman lifted Liban (and, oh, but his arms were strong!) and thrust her into his bag. Then he put the bag on his back and ran from the house with her.

Her mother ran after him. The neighbors ran with the mother. But the beggarman's legs were long and strong and his back was broad and unbending.

"Liban's in the bag, Liban's in the bag—stop him! Stop him!" cried her mother and the neighbors. But their cries only made him go faster and faster. When he came to the crossroads he laid the bag upon a bank, and he let Liban come out of it.

"Take me back to my mother," said Liban.

"Indeed, I'll do nothing of the kind," said the man, and now that he had taken off his ragged coat, and had washed his face in the stream, he looked a handsome sort of young man. "Here's a coach," he said. "It's waiting for you and me, and we'll go in it, not to the Court of Dusty Feet, but to the court in my father's castle where there will be one who will marry us. I put on the beggar's garb and carried this bag upon my back only to come to you, Liban, Beauty of Woman. There are many things I can do, but there are a few I can't do, and climbing a tree is one of them."

Then he put his arm around her and lifted her into the coach that was waiting there, with two black horses to draw it. They had just got into the coach when Liban's mother and the neighbors came up. The neighbors stopped to pick up the shower of silver that the coachman threw them, and the footman lifted Liban's mother and left her standing on the board beside him, and the coach went dashing on.

More
About Jonathan Bing

By Beatrice Curtis Brown

WHY do you sit by yourself in the sun,
  Jonathan Bing, Jonathan Bing?
Why do you sit by yourself in the sun,
When you know there is plenty of work to be done,
  Jonathan, Jonathan Bing?"

"Why, do you ask, by myself do I sit?"
  Said Jonathan Bing, Jonathan Bing.
"The question is foolish, as you must admit,
  For there's no one, I think, that can *help* you to sit,"
  Said Jonathan, Jonathan Bing.

35

"Why do you sit on the floor, if you please,
Jonathan Bing, Jonathan Bing?
Why do you sit on the floor,
if you please,
Holding a dining-room chair
on your knees,
Jonathan, Jonathan Bing?"

"For sixty-odd years, without any mishap,"
Said Jonathan Bing, Jonathan Bing,
"This chair has supported
my weight on its lap;
Now it's sitting on me
while it takes a short nap,"
Said Jonathan, Jonathan Bing.

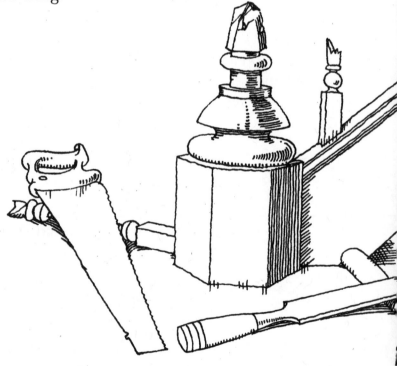

"What are you making that racket about,
    Jonathan Bing, Jonathan Bing?
What are you chipping
    and chopping about,
Why are you taking
    that staircase out,
Jonathan, Jonathan Bing?"

"I'm turning it up so it stands on its head,"
    Said Jonathan Bing, Jonathan Bing.
"So the stairs will go *down*
    when I go up to bed,
And if they go *up*
    when I come down, instead,
What matter?" said Jonathan Bing.

St. Valentine

By Eunice Tietjens

I'M SURE I don't know who he was,
The saint whose name was Valentine;
Nor what he could have done to cause
A holiday like yours and mine.

But this I do know: he was kind,
And people loved him near and far;
So when he died they had a mind
To keep him in the calendar.

He must have been a man who knew
A lot of secrets everywhere
But never told—just laughed and drew
A frilly pattern in the air.

And when at dusk he walked the town,
Shy lovers courtesied as he passed,
And children, as the dark came down,
Ran to his hand and held it fast.

39

Story Tell

By Laura E. Richards

He held his pipkin up
  a minute,
And down they fell,
  all ready, in it.

"T ELL me about
  a funny old man!"
"And so I will!
  His name was Dan.
He lived in the town
  of Wumpston Wells
In a home made out
  of oyster shells.
The oysters hung
  about inside,
And when he wanted
  some, broiled or fried,

"The chairs were made
  of peanut brittle,
Yes, every one,
  both big and little;
The cushions all
  of plummy cake;
And—" "Did it make
  his tummy ache?"
"It did, my dear!
  The wisest plan
Will be to say
  no more of Dan."

40

ABOUT a funny
   old woman, then!"
"Well! *She*—her name
   was Hepzibah N.
What is N. for?
   For Ninnycumtwitch,
Or Niddlecum dinky,
   I don't know which—
The funny thing
   about her was
She never could hold
   her tongue, because
'Twas hung in the middle
   and wagged at both ends,
A serious trial
   to all her friends;

"For when they wanted
   to ask her to dinner,
They had to gag her,
   as I'm a sinner.
Then she would go home
   in a terrible huff
And say she hadn't
   had half enough;
And they would say,
   'Oh!'—
and then—
   and then
I think
   that's enough
about
   Hepzibah N."

Robert Lawson.

"THEN tell—oh, tell
    about an ogre!"
"Well! There was one
    who wore a toga.
He said, 'It is
    the proper fashion!'
He went into
    a frightful passion

Because his uncles
    and the rest
Still clung to trousers,
    coat, and vest.
He gnashed his teeth;
    he screamed and roared
Until his uncles
    all were bored.

"They wopsed him up
    within his toga
And sent him off
    to Saratoga.
I've heard no further
    word about him,
But we do very well
    without him.
And now, my child,
    whatever hap,
I *must* go up
    and take my nap!"

42

The Little Dragon

By Constance Savery

THERE was once a little dragon, quite nice and tame. His name was Augustus, and he lived with his father and mother in a cave with colored icicles hanging from the roof.

As the little dragon could not fly very far, he often had to stay at home in the cave on the hillside, coiled round three times, watching the people who passed in the valley far below. He liked watching the boys and girls and market folk, but when the prince rode by in golden armor on his coal-black steed, the poor little dragon nearly cried.

"I wish I were a prince," thought he. "How fine I should look in that flashing armor on that black horse! Oh, I do wish I were a prince!"

"Well, so you are a prince," said the old gypsy woman who had come softly up the hillside to the entrance of the cave. "But you are under a spell cast by those wicked dragons who are pretending to be your father and mother. They turned their dragon-son into a prince, and they turned you into a dragon and took you to live in their cave."

"But why did they do it?" asked the little dragon.

"Ah, it's a fine thing to have a prince for your son,"

laughed the gypsy woman. "Mr. and Mrs. Dragon always were ambitious."

"Can't I undo the spell?" said the little dragon.

"You might," said the gypsy. "Take a crystal bowl, fill it with powdered sea shells steeped in elderberry cordial, and drink deep. That should serve you."

Then the gypsy woman hobbled away. She did not mean to tell an untruth, but unfortunately she had made a sad mistake in thinking that Mr. and Mrs. Dragon had cast a spell on their little Augustus. They had done no such thing.

The little dragon felt angry and important. He puffed out his chest at the thought that he was really the prince who owned the white, shining palace down in the valley. "I will undo the spell at once," he said.

So he waddled down to the shore and gathered sea shells and pounded them with his mother's flatiron and steeped them in elderberry cordial. Next he poured the mixture into a crystal bowl, and last of all he drank it. He also swallowed the flatiron quite by mistake, which was perhaps the reason why the spell was not undone. For he was still a little dragon.

When the gypsy woman came again, the little dragon was very cross with her.

"Your spell was worse than useless," said he. "And Mother was dreadfully vexed about her flatiron."

The gypsy woman was sorry for him. "I will tell you other remedies," she said.

And she gave him seven more spells for undoing spells, but none of them was any good. The little dragon slept on young green nettles for nine nights, and ate toadstools gathered from thirteen fairy rings, and washed in sea foam mixed with May dew, and drank four potions, each more horrible than the last—but nothing would turn him into a prince. At last he grew tired of trying spells. One day the prince rode past the cave on his black horse, and at once Augustus pounced on him and dragged him inside.

The prince was not expecting to be pounced on. He was so much taken by surprise that he did not even try to fight the little dragon.

"Now I've got you, wicked creature!" said Augustus. "You're not a prince at all. You're the son of the dragons that live in this cave. I am the real prince under a spell."

"Absurd!" said the prince, as bravely as he could.

"It isn't absurd," said Augustus indignantly. "Take off your armor and your clothes. I am going down to my palace. You must stay here."

The prince struggled hard, but Augustus was the stronger of the two. He tore away all the beautiful golden armor the prince had on and most of the prince's clothes. And then Augustus dressed himself for his arrival at the palace.

It took him three hours to dress and don his armor. Everything was so small that he had to fasten himself together with pieces of string and many safety pins. The prince sulked in a corner, refusing to help.

As soon as Augustus was dressed, he locked the door of the cave behind him, left the key in the lock, and marched down to the palace. The courtiers and servants were just setting out in search of their gallant prince, who had not returned from hunting in the hills. The sight of the little dragon made them run away screaming.

"Do not be afraid, my friends," said Augustus. "I am your unhappy master under a spell."

So they came timidly up to him, and he was led into the palace.

Meanwhile the prince sat in the cave with colored icicles, wondering what would happen when Mr. and Mrs. Dragon came back from their ride through the air. At midnight he heard the beating of their great wings.

"And pray, who are you?" said Mr. Dragon in surprise.

"I am the prince of this country," answered the young man. "Your son dragged me into this cave and robbed me of my armor and my clothes, saying that he was the true prince. A gypsy woman had told him so. He has gone to my palace to take possession of it."

"So that's what was the matter with Augustus!" said Mrs. Dragon. "I could see that the silly child had something on his mind, but I couldn't find out what was troubling him. He thinks he's a prince under a spell, does he? Ha, ha, ha!"

"I should like to go home now," said the prince politely.

"You can't," said Mrs. Dragon. "Not like that! It is beneath your dignity to go to your palace in the few rags Augustus has left you. I would make you some new clothes if I could," she added kindly, "but unluckily I am not good at sewing. My claws always catch in the stuff."

"You had better stay with us until Augustus returns," said Mr. Dragon. "He'll come home sooner or later. He's not cut out for a prince. He, he, he! Have some supper?"

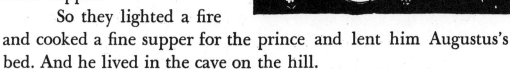

So they lighted a fire and cooked a fine supper for the prince and lent him Augustus's bed. And he lived in the cave on the hill.

As for Augustus, he sat on a tight, uncomfortable golden throne, dressed in glorious robes. All day long tailors were running sharp pins into him as they tried on his new court clothes. At night he slept in the state bed, which was so much too small for him that he often rolled out of it with a terrible bump on the floor. And at mealtimes he never had enough to eat. When he cleared the gold and silver dishes, his courtiers whispered to one another, "What a greedy appetite his Highness has!"

One day he was sitting by himself in the gardens of the palace, a lonely little dragon. His subjects believed that he was their prince, but they were always afraid that a prince under a dragon spell might be tempted to snap. So they left him alone.

He looked up, and there stood the gypsy woman.

"How are you getting on?" she inquired.

"Not very well," said the little dragon.

"The prince is getting on very well indeed," said the gypsy. "He likes his life in the cave. At night your mother and father take him out treasure-hunting. He sits on your father's back, holding his scaly wings. They went to the mountains of the moon last night

47

to gather moonstones. And you should see the emeralds he brought back from the shores of the sea that no man knows!"

"Oh!" said the little dragon.

"Then they come back and make a huge fire of dried ferns and pine cones and sea wood, and your mother cooks the supper. Plum porridge! Great big platefuls!"

"Oh!" said the little dragon. "Oh!"

"And when the dishes are washed and shining dry, your mother and father sing to him—scales and catches and snatches."

"Oh!" said the little dragon. "Oh, oh, oh!"

And he asked anxiously, "Does my mother—Mrs. Dragon, I mean—does she like him better than me?"

The gypsy woman only laughed.

Late that night Mr. and Mrs. Dragon heard a whimpering and sniffling outside the cave. They looked out and saw

Augustus. In his claws he held clothes and a suit of armor for the prince.

"Oh, Mother, let me in!" he cried. "I want to come home. I don't believe that gypsy woman spoke the truth. I would rather be a dragon than a prince."

"You are much better fitted to be a dragon than a prince, Augustus," said his mother severely. "Come in at once, and don't let me hear any more nonsense."

So Augustus came in and sat down. The prince began to dress himself in his splendid clothes and glittering armor. He looked every inch a prince as he buckled on his sword. Then he drew it from the scabbard and bade Mr. Dragon kneel.

"I wish to reward you for your services," he said.

Mr. Dragon knelt as well as he could for his tail.

The prince struck him lightly on the shoulder and said, "Rise, Sir Dragon."

Then he said good-by rather coldly to Augustus, climbed onto Sir Dragon's back, and was swiftly borne home to the palace. Lady Dragon went, too, carrying the moonstones and emeralds.

Augustus stayed at home and washed the dishes, after he had eaten all that was left of the good supper. Then he crawled into his large bed, saying to himself, "It's better to be a dragon than a prince. There's no place like home."

And the little dragon went happily to sleep.

Planting a Tree

By Nancy Byrd Turner

FIRM in the good brown earth
　　Set we our little tree.
Clear dews will freshen it,
Cool rain will feed it,
Sun will be warming it
As warmth is needed.
Winds will blow round it free—
　　Take root, good tree!

Slowly, as days go on,
　　These boughs will stouter be.
Leaves will unfurl on them,
And, when spring comes to them,
Blossoms uncurl on them,
Birds make their homes in them,
Shade outstretch, wide and free—
　　Grow well, good tree!

50

Jonathan Bing Dances for Spring

By Beatrice Curtis Brown

BLOW the fife and clarinet,
   Let the band advance!
Mr. Bing will welcome spring
   With his festive dance!

Waking with the sunshine,
   Starting out of sleep;
Flings away the blanket gray,
   Makes a mighty leap—

Leaps upon the mantelpiece,
   Bounces up again,
Turns about and dashes out
   Through the windowpane.

All the neighbors' children
   Clap and shout "Hooray!"
When Mr. B., in highest glee,
   Comes prancing down the way.

Who can ever stop him?
   Who so fast as Bing?
When hop and prance, he does
     his dance
   To celebrate the spring.

Hop! He's on a treetop.
   Bump! He's on the tiles.
Bounce and vault and somersault,
   He goes for miles and miles.

The motor cars are hooting;
   The whistles all a-blow;
They holler "Hi!" as Bing goes by,
   "Say, where d'you think you go?"

The lord mayors of the city
   In velvet cloak and chain
Appear in state, expostulate
   With Bing—but all in vain.

"Away, you foolish creatures!"
   Cries happy Mr. Bing.
"With all this fun of flowers
      and sun
   Who would not dance
      for spring?"

Penguins

By Anne Brewer

DID you ever see a penguin?
   He flops his funny feet
And struts about and rolls his eyes
   And tries to look discreet.
But he's so very curious
   He cannot stand the strain,
So he pokes his bill in everything
   And flops his feet again.
Down there at the South Pole
With Byrd and all his men,
I didn't like the whales so much,
But, oh, the funny penguin!

He has the biggest family
  And when he takes a walk,
His aunts and all their children
  Come right along and talk.
They flip their wings and chatter
  And make the greatest fuss,
You almost think they're people,
  They act so much like us.
Down there at the South Pole
With Byrd and all his men,
I guess the blizzard's not much fun,
But, oh, the funny penguin!

55

The Piping on Christmas Eve

By Florence Page Jaques

ONCE on an island near a little town there lived a small boy called Timothy Piper. He lived all alone except for his flock of goats, and so he made willow pipes to pipe on. He lived in an old grass-grown fort at the end of the island; the goats lived just outside.

It was lucky that he liked his pipes and his goats, for no one ever came to see him, except to buy goats' milk and cheese, and even then they stayed in their boats and shouted. Timothy's grandfather, who had brought him up, had been a fierce old hermit, and forbade anyone to step foot on the island. And even after he died, people kept on not stepping.

One winter day, Timothy was sitting high up in the square tower of the fort, piping to himself. But at last he put his pipes away and looked out over the cold gray water to the town. The air was white with big soft flakes, and the red-roofed village looked very pretty through the snow screen.

"But how busy everyone is!" Timothy thought. "How fast they scurry about, and how many packages they carry! And everything seems scarlet and green and sparkly!" He leaned out the tower window. "Why, it's Christmas time!"

Timothy liked Christmas. He liked to hear the Christmas

bells across the water. And the year before a fisherman had given him an orange; the year before that someone had thrown him a red stocking full of candy! Before that Timothy could not remember. But he knew he liked Christmas. He ran down the stone steps and out to the goats. "Look here," he said to the Gray Goat, "what day is it?"

"It's the day before Christmas," said Gray Goat immediately, for he always knew the answer to everything.

"Well, look here," said Timothy breathlessly. "Do you know what I want to do? I want to go over to the village and see Christmas!"

"Why not?" said Gray Goat calmly.

Timothy looked at him in despair. Timothy had never been in the village in his life and now he had thought of doing it, and Gray Goat only stood and chewed. What a goat!

"Have you any idea how I can get over there?" Timothy asked politely.

"I'll take you over on my back, if you like," said Gray Goat. "I often swim across at night and stroll about."

Timothy looked at Gray Goat in awe. You never knew about him. You certainly never knew. But all Tim said was, "Thank you, Gray Goat." And off he started on Gray Goat's back.

The swift waves were gray and icy, and the big snowflakes drifted down across Timothy's face. It was fun. Nearer and nearer to the little town they came, and Timothy could see bright holly wreaths and gay toys, and he could hear sleigh bells somewhere and children laughing. It was terrifically exciting. He looked up to the castle that loomed above the town, and at one of its windows a little girl with yellow braids waved gaily at him!

"She waved at *me,*" Timothy told Gray Goat.

"That's the Duke's daughter," said Gray Goat. "She waves at everyone. She never has anyone to play with up there, so she waves. She even waves at me, when she catches sight of me on bright moonlight nights."

"Oh!" said Timothy.

Just then they reached the steps of the wharf, and Timothy jumped off Gray Goat's back. "Stroll around an hour or two," said Gray Goat. "I'm going to curl up in the dried grass and get warm."

Timothy ran up the steps to the street. He was more breathless than ever. There were so many things to see he simply couldn't help bumping into people as he whirled around. The shop windows, full of drums, red wagons, shining balls—things he didn't even know! Whole shops full of candy canes and caramels! Whole shops full of oranges and grapes and apples! Whole shops full of mince pies and plum puddings—oh, what a lovely smell came from those shops! And then Timothy saw a window with toy trains dashing around and around in it!

For two whole hours Timothy wandered, seeing Christmas things he had never dreamed of. He even saw a Christmas tree all hung with silver, and when they turned on the Christmas tree lights, all red and green and blue and yellow, Timothy turned somersaults with joy.

At last he happened into the square by the castle. Now this town had one queer custom; no one ever bought presents till the day before Christmas. This made shopping a rush, and people often got muddled about presents. And so to make things easier, the Duke had a list with everyone's name on it hung against the castle wall. And whoever wanted to give a certain person a present made a cross after that person's name. Then the person, on the day before Christmas, looked to see how many people were giving him pres-

ents, and bought just as many presents to give back. It *was* a queer custom, I know.

So Timothy, strolling by, saw the list.

"Whee! How many presents for the Duke's daughter!" he said, seeing the rows and rows of crosses after her name. Then he looked down the list for his own. It was there, down at the very bottom, with not a single cross after it. Timothy couldn't believe his eyes! Not a single present for him! He stood and stared.

Now it was only that people rather forgot about Timothy in the winter; they didn't really want to leave him out. But it *was* rather mean of them not to take the trouble to remember. Timothy thought so. He stood there in the snow, and his anger got fiercer and fiercer. No one was giving him a present! And there were so many everywhere! He turned on his heel and stalked back down to the wharf.

Gray Goat was waiting, and when he saw Timothy's grim face, he simply got into the water. "Nobody in this whole town is giving me a present," said Timothy bitterly. He leaped on Gray Goat's back and they sped across the stormy waves. Then Timothy went straight to his tower and began to stride up and down, kicking at the stone floor.

"At least I'm glad you're mad, instead of sad," said the Gray Goat behind him. "Your grandfather said that if you got angry at the village, I must show you your great-grandfather's pipe. Did you know he was the Pied Piper?"

61

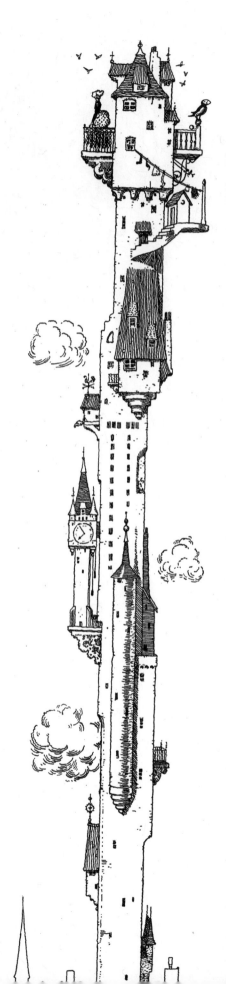

"The one who could make anything follow him by piping? Who piped away the rats and the children from Hamelin town?" asked Timothy, quite round-eyed.

"His pipe is there on the high shelf," said Gray Goat, and then he went softly away.

Timothy sat and looked at the shelf. It was twilight, and only a few flakes of snow were falling now, outside. Timothy lifted the pipe of the Pied Piper of Hamelin down from the shelf.

"But—how can you know whom you are calling?" he wondered, and blew a few notes. A queer feeling came over him when he found he was making a little tune of his own. He played it over and over, and suddenly he heard a pattering. The whole flock of goats came rushing into the room.

"No, no!" said Timothy. "I certainly didn't mean to bring you here! I can see you any time!"

So he tried another tune. And outside the window, flap, flap, he saw silverfish jump from the water and come bouncing to his steps. "No, no! I don't want you!" he called, and stopped playing at once. The fish sank back with sighs of relief into the water.

"I'll have to play a far-away tune, to reach the town," Timothy thought. "And I know! I'll try to play the kind of tune that will bring all the Christmas presents over here! What a joke!"

He waited by his window till he saw the candles in the town go out, one by one. When everything was dark and still, he picked up his pipe and began to play once more, a queer little, bright little tune. He made it as queer as he could, for he didn't want to pipe the children over! That would have been too cruel a joke.

Soon he actually heard faint noises over in the town, doors opening, and shuffling sounds. What *was* stirring? There was a faint moon, and at last he thought he saw something moving down by the wharf. Then he saw boats putting off, boat after boat!

"Oh, I *hope* the Christmas presents are coming!" Timothy thought. "And if not, *what* is?"

He piped on and on. He could hear the boats landing and he heard Gray Goat say, "Ho, ho! Well, of *all* things!" ("Then it isn't the Christmas presents," thought Timothy.) "Come along; this way!"

Timothy rushed down to throw open the door of the fort, piping all the while.

Then into the big hall came the strangest procession! Turkeys and plum puddings, cakes and candies, potatoes, celery, sacks of sugar, raisins, pumpkin pies, mince pies, roast beef, cranberries—in fact, every single thing to eat that there was in the whole town came marching into Timothy's hall. It was a surprising sight.

Timothy gasped. Then he caught Gray Goat's eye, and they both began to laugh.

"You *have* played a joke this time!" said Gray Goat. "Not bad! Not bad at all! Just wait till they find out over there! But now you'd better go off to sleep."

63

Timothy was still asleep next morning when Gray Goat prodded him. He seemed very excited.

"Wake up, Timothy," Gray Goat said. "There are boats and boats below. Even one with the Duke himself in it. It seems his daughter was looking at the moon last night and saw the Christmas dinners all taking off to the island."

"Shall I go down?" said Timothy.

"I took the liberty," said Gray Goat, "of telling the Duke that we couldn't possibly return the dinners when they'd come here of their own accord. But that you would be glad to have everyone come here and have dinner with us. Only, of course, to be polite, they would each bring along a Christmas present for you."

"Gray Goat," said Timothy, with his hair standing up in delight, "what a goat you are!"

And what a good time everyone had, having Christmas dinner all together, in Timothy's hall! Even the Duke and the Duke's daughter came, with presents tied up in gold tissue. And after dinner they all sang carols, and Timothy opened his presents, three hundred and thirty-three of them, and the Duke's daughter helped him, and so did all the other children.

So after that the children often came to the island to play with Timothy, and his presents, and his goats. The Duke's daughter came specially often, and Timothy went to visit her in her castle, too, so she no longer had to sit waving all alone at her window!

But Timothy put his great-grandfather's pipe back on the high shelf again. It was exciting to pipe on a pipe like that, but you never could be sure what *might* happen.